BLACK GIRL YOU ARE ATLAS

A *USA Today* Bestseller

A *Kirkus* Best Book of the Year

A *School Library Journal* Best Book of the Year

A *Horn Book* Best Book of the Year

A 2025 NCTE Notable Verse Novel

A *BookPage* Best Young Adult Book of the Year

An NPR Book We Love of 2024

A *Cosmopolitan* Best Young Adult Book of 2024

A New York Public Library Best Book of 2024

A Chicago Public Library Best Book of 2024

A Center for the Study of Multicultural Children's Literature Best Book of 2024

A Common Sense Media Best Book of 2024

A National Education Association Read Across America 2024–2025 Selection

★ "[A] moving, introspective poetry collection celebrating the possibilities of Black girlhood complemented by atmospheric mixed-media illustrations ... A compelling ode to self-resurrection and Black sisterhood." —*Kirkus Reviews*, starred review

★ "Brimming with vibrant, layered poetry and stunningly textured collage art, this ballad for Black girls is a must for all collections ... The combination of poetry and collage art is exceptionally powerful and dynamic." —*School Library Journal*, starred review

★ "This poetry collection masterfully encapsulates Watson's experience of Black girlhood and womanhood ... The collaboration with Holmes, whose magnificent collages accompany Watson's words, adds a visual dimension that also spans cultures and experiences. The result is a celebration of the complexities of, and the bonds formed through, Black girlhood and womanhood."

—*The Horn Book*, starred review

★ "Watson offers high-impact, widely accessible poems ... a phenomenal poetry collection celebrating sisterhood, womanhood, Black culture, and the power of family and friendship ... Caldecott Honor recipient Holmes's torn paper collage and mixed-media art is the perfect accompaniment ... Shimmering with radiance."

—*BookPage*, starred review

"[A] semi-autobiographical collection that speaks to ... the expansive experience of Black girlhood as it cycles toward womanhood via sharp and loving poetry. Accompanied by striking and vintage-feeling multimedia collage artwork ... [this is] a tender ode to universal yearnings for safety, love, and justice, as well as a celebration of Black girlhood." —*Publishers Weekly*

"Watson's latest collection of poetry is a powerful mixture of free verse and short-form poetry ... The poems are accompanied by Holmes's breathtaking collage art." —*Booklist*

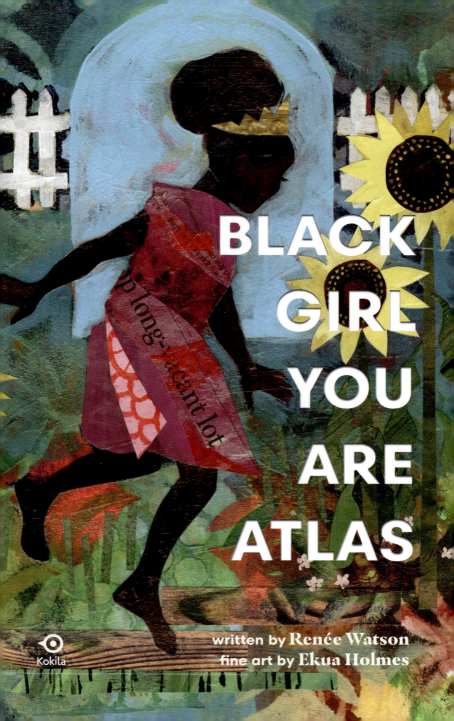

KOKILA
An imprint of Penguin Random House LLC
1745 Broadway, New York, New York 10019

First published in the United States of America by Kokila,
an imprint of Penguin Random House LLC, 2024
First paperback edition published 2025

Text copyright © 2024 by Renée Watson
Fine art copyright © 2024 by Ekua Holmes

Penguin Random House values and supports copyright. Copyright fuels creativity, encourages diverse voices, promotes free speech, and creates a vibrant culture. Thank you for buying an authorized edition of this book and for complying with copyright laws by not reproducing, scanning, or distributing any part of it in any form without permission. You are supporting writers and allowing Penguin Random House to continue to publish books for every reader. Please note that no part of this book may be used or reproduced in any manner for the purpose of training artificial intelligence technologies or systems.

Kokila & colophon are registered trademarks of Penguin Random House LLC.
The Penguin colophon is a registered trademark of Penguin Books Limited.

Visit us online at PenguinRandomHouse.com.

The Library of Congress has cataloged the hardcover edition as follows:
Names: Watson, Renée, author. | Holmes, Ekua, illustrator.
Title: Black girl you are Atlas / written by Renée Watson; fine art by Ekua Holmes.
Description: New York: Kokila, 2024. | Summary: "Poet Renée Watson looks back at her childhood and urges readers to look forward at their futures with love, understanding, and celebration in this fully illustrated poetry collection"—Provided by publisher.
Identifiers: LCCN 2023022527 (print) | LCCN 2023022528 (ebook) | ISBN 9780593461709 | ISBN 9780593461716 (ebook)
Subjects: LCSH: African American girls—Poetry. | African American women—Poetry. | American poetry. | LCGFT: Autobiographical poetry.
Classification: LCC PS3623.A87335 B58 2024 (print) | LCC PS3623.A87335 (ebook) | DDC 811/.6—dc23/eng/20230925
LC record available at https://lccn.loc.gov/2023022527
LC ebook record available at https://lccn.loc.gov/2023022528

Printed in China

ISBN 9780593461723

10 9 8 7 6 5 4 3 2 1

TOPL

This book was edited by Namrata Tripathi and designed by Jasmin Rubero.
The production was supervised by Tabitha Dulla, Nicole Kiser, Ariela Rudy Zaltzman, and Cherisse Landau.

Text set in Masqualero

The art for this book was selected from the collages of Ekua Holmes and includes two pieces done specifically for this project. Each mixed-media piece includes cut and torn papers that were found, created, painted, and prepared, along with photos and drawings.

This book is a work of fiction. Any references to historical events, real people, or real places are used fictitiously. Other names, characters, places, and events are products of the author's imagination, and any resemblance to actual events or places or persons, living or dead, is entirely coincidental.

The publisher does not have any control over and does not assume any responsibility for author or third-party websites or their content.

The authorized representative in the EU for product safety and compliance is Penguin Random House Ireland, Morrison Chambers, 32 Nassau Street, Dublin D02 YH68, Ireland, https://eu-contact.penguin.ie.

In Loving Memory of Kamilah Aisha Moon
1973–2021

*Your need is over,
but your giving goes on
& on.*

—Kamilah Aisha Moon, "Disbelief"

Where I'm From
after Willie Perdomo

I'm made up of east coast hip-hop and island tradition.
I'm from Baptist hymns and secular jigs.
Tambourine playin', late night stayin'
at the church house, or my friend's house, or their friend's house
(on the weekends).

Where I'm from there are corduroyed hand-me-downs
and family keepsakes. Family pictures on the wall.
Open Bible on the coffee table.

I'm from that side of town.
Where the media only comes for bloodshed. Blood wasted.
Never for blood restored, celebrated, regenerated.

I'm from hopscotch and Double Dutch.
From hide-n-seek and Pac-Man.
I'm from curry goat, rice and peas, and beef patties.
From turquoise-blue water, white sand, and dreadlocks.
Reggae is in my blood.

I'm from the Pacific Northwest.
A place where rain falls more than sun shines.
I'm from Douglas firs and pine trees.
Where we walk under waterfalls,

drive up windy roads to Mt. Hood,
and escape to the beaches on the Oregon coast.

Where I'm from music takes away the blues.
I'm from Bob Marley. Mahalia Jackson.
Aretha Franklin. James Brown.
I'm from Jackson 5 records and New Edition tapes.
Where I'm from we rewind tapes over and over
and over again so we can write down the lyrics
and memorize them.

Where I'm from the whole neighborhood is your family:
ladies sit on their porches looking out for you,
shooin' away boys like flies,
callin' your momma to tell her what you did
before you can get home and lie about it.

Where I'm from people ask my friend,
"Is that your hair?" and she says, "Yeah, it's mine. I bought it!"

I'm from divorce being passed down to children
like a family heirloom.
From single mommas pushing strollers,
praying that their babies don't have the same struggles as them.

I'm from a little goes a long way,
from sun's gonna shine after the rain.

I'm from perseverin' souls and hardworkin' hands.
From a people destined to make it to their promised land.
I'm from been there, done that, can and will do it again.
Now you tell me—where you from?

Resurrection

She named me Renée.

Renée, the name that means rebirth, to bring new life.
Maybe she named me this because I came last,
her fifth child born just before the death of her marriage.
Maybe I was prophecy that she'd live again. Without him.

Of all the hand-me-downs bestowed on me,
my name is not one of them. Roy has my father's name,
and Cheryl was named by our grandmother.
Trisa shares her middle name, Elizabeth, with our mom,
and Dyan was named after Dyan Cannon
because our father liked the spelling: D Y A N.

But there is no family history, no special tale tied to my name.
It is all mine. An abracadabra name. Renée.
The name of new beginnings, the name for demolishing
and building back up.

My name is the R&B slow jam
about the love who left and came back,
is the Sunday morning hallelujah, is the protest chant,
is the Second Line.

My name carries the strength of Grandma Roberta,
who died before I got to say goodbye,
before I understood that grandmothers, like flowers,
always die too soon.

To write my name is to spell the sorrows of my ancestors,
how they were sold and traded, hanged and drowned.
How their tears and sweat and blood seeded generations.

To say my name is to pronounce resilience,
is to have a bounce-back accent
on the tip of your tongue.

To say my name is to hold a prayer, a second chance.
Is to count me out, watch me rise.

a black girl gives thanks

for the aunties by blood & by choice
who knew how to give warning
by look or clearing throat
or sitting forward just enough
to get the point across

for every peppermint candy
& Werther's Original
smuggled from hand to hand
on Sunday mornings

for hand-clapping games
& Hula-Hoops & roller skates
& brown baby dolls
& brown angels on top of Christmas trees

for all the gossip swirling 'round
too-young ears at the family gathering
for the prayers and warnings
for the advice asked for
& advice given anyway

for pressing combs & royal crown hair grease
for brown hands that braid & twist thick tresses

for the way *giiirr*l is song
is confirmation
is chastisement
is prayer

for cornbread & honey butter
& always a crockpot
holding home

for freedom fighters & protest poets
for every tale passed down
that tells the story
that we survived
how we survived

oh give thanks
oh give thanks

Sisterhood Haiku, I

And what would we do
without the knowing women?
How could we survive?

How Sisters Love
for Dyan

To understand my sister's love
you must know that in Portland
snow turns to black ice
and slides cars into tree trunks.

You must know that I am
scared of anything new
and snow for me was new
because I was only three when we left Paterson
and my tiny feet didn't know snow.

You must know that this winter was a bad winter,
one the news reported about.
This snow was big snow,
inches upon inches upon inches,
and my sister and I got caught out in the storm.

You must know that I was maybe six or
an age like six and she was eleven
or something like eleven
when she told me,
Hold on to the back of my coat, tight. Don't let go.
Walk in my footsteps.

And she plunged her feet
into ice-cold snow mountains,
pushed them to ground
and made a path for me.

This, you have to know
to understand
us.

Altars

Every girl growing into woman
needs a porch or stoop
or backyard-swing or altar.
Needs to learn how to be alone,
how to watch,
watch and wait.

Needs to learn how to be in harmony
with the music of her breath.

Every girl growing into woman
needs a teapot, a crockpot.
Needs to learn how to slow down,
slow down and wait.

Needs to learn how to steep,
how to take her time, simmer to a boil.

at·las | \ 'at-les \
from Merriam-Webster Dictionary

1 *capitalized:*
a Titan who for his part in the Titans' revolt
against the gods is forced by Zeus
to support the heavens on his shoulders

2 *capitalized:* one who bears a heavy burden

3(a): a bound collection of maps
often including illustrations,
informative tables, or textual matter

Black girl you are Atlas. The way you carry the weight of the hood on your shoulders like a too-heavy backpack. How you big-sister the Black boys on the playground, in the classroom, in the back row of the choir stand who need a good stare-down every now and then. You already know when to tell your friend, *He ain't the one for you.* You already know she won't listen and you will be there to wipe her tears when love fails her. Black girl you are Atlas. The way your very presence in a room is a reminder of where you come from, a demand of what you are owed. Black girl you are atlas. Your bones a collection of histories, your blood rivers and flows, rivers and flows. You carry the dirges, the wailing. You carry the requiem of your ancestors, you are proof of their sweet breath. You queened and ruled and slaved and plowed and escaped and fought and got captured and fought and marched and protested and raised funds and raised fists and fought and fought and passed out flyers and voted in and voted out and fought and fought for your rights, for your peace of mind, for today, for tomorrow. Black girl you are atlas. You carry the jig and the two-step. You are festival and feast. You are nourishment in famine. Black girl you are atlas. You know the way back, the way forward. Black girl you are Atlas. The way no one expected you to be the fulfillment of prophecy. But it is you, always, who holds the world up.

That Girl

Ooh, look at that girl.
You see the way she walk?
Like she got somewhere to be.
No.
Like she tryin' to leave?
Yeah.
She walkin' fast, like she gotta get away
and never come back.
Walkin' from a dark past, a few mistakes.
That girl look like she walkin' from a home
that don't know she gone,
or that just don't care.

You see that girl's eyes?
Her eyes look empty.
Look like they were once full of tears,
but she done let the tears go.
Look like she can't cry no more,
even if she wanted to.
Look like she can't laugh no more
but sounds like she tries to.
I hear her gigglin' on the street corner,
flirtin' with those boys.
So good at pretendin', she almost believes her smile.
So good at pretendin', they almost believe it too.

That girl.

That girl used to have innocent moments
playin' Simon Says on school playgrounds.
That girl used to sit on the porch swing at Big Momma's house
eatin' watermelon from a tin pan.
So naïve that she would save the seeds
so she could plant them later.

That girl.

That girl done changed.
She done got older and started realizin'
that people break promises and forget to say sorry.
That girl. That girl done changed.
She done got older and started realizin'
that she's growin' up to be just like her mother,
even though she don't want to be.
Can't help it. That girl.
She wants to get away. Out of this city.
Start over.
Have a new reputation.
An erased past.

That girl wants to move to a place
where the watermelon she eats is seedless
so there will be no disappointment from fruitless harvests.

Sisterhood Haiku, II

The wise women know
nothing can heal without love,
no growth without care.

Love Shows Up

When mommas and aunties ask, *Have you eaten?*
When the old men say, *Alright now* as you walk by.
Love shows up when your friend drags out, O*kaaay* and tells you,
You wearin' that outfit today.
When your grandma saves leftovers and puts your initials
on the takeout container so no one eats your food.

Love shows up in the light left on above the stove
in case you wake in the middle of the night
and need to find your way.

Love shows up in the giggles spilling out of a toddler being tickled,
in the head nod from a stranger passing by,
in the glance from a friend from across the room
who knows exactly what you're thinking.

Love shows up in winter's first snowfall that kisses the ground,
in the cooling breeze at the end of a hot, humid day.

Love shows up in spring when the leaves return to trees,
keeping their promise that they'd be back.

Love comes back.
Love shows up.
Love shows
love.

Church of Press & Curl

On Saturdays, Ms. Tiny's kitchen
becomes the House of Miracles.
She baptizes my hair,
washing its sin down the drain of her basin.

She is the bishop of blow-dry
bringing comb to root as hot heat tunnels through follicles.
Her pressing comb rests on a towel by the stove,
a dollop of Blue Magic hair grease on the top of her hand
ready to oil scalp, anoint it.

Smoke from the iron comb sends up an offering.
Each strand of hair surrenders its will,
falls to my shoulders in repentance.

And I am made anew
and my Shirley Temple curls testify
and boys say it's pretty
and Black girls pull it to see if it's real
and white girls want to touch it
and grown-ups make me promise to never cut it
and for one week my hair's soul is regenerated.

But when the rain comes
my curls backslide

and Africa proves stronger
than any metal comb,
than any silk scarf,
than any sponge rollers.

My sinner hair won't obey assimilation,
won't convert, no longer obedient
to Ms. Tiny's ole-time religion.
It is born again, made anew.
Free.

Scalp
response to Atiai, 1970 by J.D. 'Okhai Ojeikere

Plowing through naps
like cotton fields.
Each pathway a map
to the underground railroad.

Black cotton gathered, pulled.
Every handful a testimony.

Bundle this majesty.
Part it, twist it, braid it.
Sculpt it into a crown. Holy.

Turning Seven

i

My birthday is spent on an Amtrak train somewhere between Oregon and New Jersey. Mom and Aunt Mary tell the attendants, and the conductor makes an announcement over the intercom. Passengers sing "Happy Birthday" to me, and throughout the day, people walk by waving and shaking my hand, asking if they can give me a hug. An old man gives me seven single-dollar bills, one for each year. One of the attendants brings me a coloring book and a warm brownie with two scoops of vanilla ice cream. The candle isn't lit but I blow anyway.

ii

I wish for a bigger house so me and my three sisters can each have our own rooms, for Mom to have enough money so she'll never have to hold up the line again cashing in coupons, for name-brand shoes instead of Pro Wings, for this trip to be a good trip because this is the trip I am seeing my father. The last time I saw him I was three and I don't remember him or know him but I want to.

iii
Mom and Dad are handling grown-folks business in the living room. Signing papers, arguing words I do not know, have never heard: *House deed. Sale. Mortgage.* I sit with Grandma Agatha. When I look into her eyes, I see Jamaica. And not the tourist waters and hammocks and drums, but Jamaica machete, Jamaica blues.

iv
She pours me a fizzing ginger ale in a clear glass. We sit in the kitchen, pretend we don't hear my mom and dad yelling. She asks me, "What are your birthday wishes?" I tell her I want a Strawberry Shortcake bike and a Cabbage Patch doll because that is what seven-year-old girls should wish for.

v
When we get back to Portland, my mother throws me a belated birthday party. I have been seven for one whole week and I get my bike and doll, and we barbecue in the backyard. There is music and my favorite lemon cake and the yard is full of cousins and schoolmates and churchmates and we dance and eat and pin the tail and hide and seek and slip and slide until the sun goes down.

The boys leave, but the girls stay.

A slumber party with no sleep. And I have forgotten what it felt like when my dad called me chubby, when he pinched my cheeks and asked, "What is your momma feeding you?" And it doesn't matter now that he didn't have time to look at the coloring book a stranger gave me. And it doesn't matter that he didn't give me anything. I am with Akiba, Karen, Tenisha, and Clairvetta. I am seven and I am told this is a lucky number.

But then the phone rings before the sun rises, and my mom holds the receiver to her ear while tears fall.

Uncle Frank has died, and he is the uncle who was funny and gave me the good kind of Popsicles, the ones that never dry out. He is the human spaceship that puts you on his shoulders and runs you through the sky so that the wind can kiss every part of your face. My aunt kisses his face in the casket. I look away, wonder if I will ever be touched by the sky again.

vi
I will always remember this birthday as the one where I met my dad and lost my uncle and learned that men are good at disappointing and disappearing.

vii
I close my eyes,
wish to be six again
or eight.

Penny Fountain

Wish for wisdom to accompany knowledge,
for grace to be a confidant,
for renewal to be constant.

Wish for time well spent, for time to be respected
as the limited resource it is.

Wish for healing in the invisible, aching places.
Wish for someone to love you the way you need it.

Wish for no need
for wishes, for no prayer to go
unanswered.

Lessons on Being a Sky Walker

When they tell you
the sky is the limit, vow to go past that.
Spend your days hopscotching across clouds
from dream to   dream.
Land on the sun, rest on the moon.

Stretch, stretch,   stretch
till you reach the star tucked away in the corner of the onyx sky.
Hold the galaxy in your fingertips,
do not make a wish—
make yourself.

Build a new world
somewhere above the horizon
above your past, above your fears
far away from the naysayers,
somewhere there   there
reach your zenith

and never come down.

When I Say I Love Us

What I'm saying is I love how we cock our heads to the side,
give the stare down of all stare downs
when we really mean business.

What I'm saying is I love how saying *You good?*
has countless meanings depending on how we ask it.

When I say I love us, what I'm saying is I love
how we stop what we're doing when our song comes on,
how we sing with our whole bodies.

When I say I love us, what I mean is
I love our cornrows and fades,
Bantu knots and locs.
I mean I love our press & curl,
our afro and twist out
and bald and low cut and
braids and beads and bonnet and du-rag.

I mean I love, love our bounce back
our clap back,
our backbone,
our backstory,
our comeback.

We go way back.
Our history dripping
and damp from ocean waves.

I mean I love our resistance,
love our resilience.

I mean I love us loving us.
I mean I love loving us.
I mean I love the love that is us.

Turning Thirteen

Rodney King has been beaten by LAPD police officers
and I can't stop thinking about the cute boy at school
who asked me, *Why are you so beautiful?*

Rodney King has been beaten by LAPD police officers
and I can't stop wondering if one day the cute Black boy at school
will also be beaten or disappear or die
at the hands of police or white supremacists
like so many Black boys, Black men, do.

Whitney Houston and Janet Jackson
validate my crush on the cute Black boy
who makes honor roll and blows me a kiss
when he walks onto the stage to get his certificate.
I sing with Whitney and Janet all night in the mirror
about the cute, smart Black boy being *all the man that I'll ever need*,
and how *love will never do without* him.

Miles Davis has died and the cute, smart
Black boy invites me over
to study with a group of friends, he says.
But when I get there, no friends are there
and no parent either and he turns the radio on
to a jazz station trying to set a mood

my momma warned me about
so I leave.

Mariah Carey understands me. And Boyz II Men sing everything
I want to hear from the cute, smart, jazz-loving Black boy
who now has a girlfriend who is not me.

And I can't stop thinking about Anita Hill
and how she has to speak her trauma to a nation.
Can't stop wondering if I should tell someone
about the cute, smart, jazz-loving Black boy
who keeps touching my butt and blowing me kisses
(even though he has a girlfriend),
(even though I tell him to stop).

And thirteen holds protests and riots,
R&B and jazz, homework and study hall,
tender kisses and unwanted touch.

And when I blow out
thirteen candles on a hot July day
my siblings and cousins and friends say,
Make a wish as if wishing can give
a Black girl what she needs to survive.

Underbelly

Black girl body be ship weathering storm.
Black girl body be lighthouse.
Black girl body be cumulous cloud.
Black girl body be ore.
Black girl body be shelter.
Black girl body be temple.
Black girl body be holy, holy.
Black girl body be tambourine.
Black girl body be windstorm.
Black girl body be gentle breeze.
Black girl body be sunrise.
Black girl body be avalanche of tears.
Black girl body be cloak of giggles.
Black girl body be galaxy of prayers.
Black girl body be harvest.
Black girl body be shimmy-shimmy.
Black girl body be shake-shake.
Black girl body be rhythm.
Black girl body be blues.

Turning Sweet Sixteen

But what if I want to be sour? What if when you ask me, *How are you?*
I tell you the truth. I am not fine all the time.

Sometimes I cry myself to sleep to drown out the moaning
of my eighty-five-year-old grandfather who is losing his mind,
can't remember my name, is afraid of me
when I come home unannounced.

Sometimes I am jealous of the thinner, lighter girls who can shop
at any store with their just-right waists and just-right breasts and
just-right hips. Sometimes I am worried about my family:
Do we have enough money? Will I come home from school
one day and find my grandfather dead? How much more hardship
can my mother take before she breaks?

One day, while walking home by myself, minding my business,
minding my mind. Turning these questions into prayers:
God, please help us... A voice calls out to me but he is not God.
Yells out, *A pretty girl like you ought to be smiling.*
Tells me, *Men don't want no woman who look so mean.*

And so, I learn how to keep a twinkle in my eye,
just after a good cry. Learn how to toss my sorrow
in the ocean of my laughter.

How to bury every fear in the crater of my smile.
I know how to be sweet, I do.

And I know very well
that too-sweet things cause decay,
rot you from the inside out.

Sixteen Reasons to Smile

Sunrises
Hugs
Dulce de leche ice cream
Long walks
A timeless playlist
The smell of a new book
Hours roaming a museum
Shopping at street markets
Bar-b-que
Family Movie Night
Snuggling in a handmade quilt
Comfortable shoes
Hot tea with a splash of cream
Road trips
Hair, freshly washed
The endless song of waves crashing

King
for Roy

And my brother is the first man to love me.
Calls me baby girl, tells me I am beautiful.
Picks me up from my crib when the pacifier has fallen
out of my mouth, when I am overwhelmed with tears.

And my brother is the first man I see cry,
first man I know who is not afraid or ashamed
of his tears, is not too proud to say,
I love you or *I'm sorry.*

And my brother is the first man to send me letters
in the mail while he is away with the marines,
away from all the women he loves,
all the women who love him. His momma and four sisters.
I think he loves me most. Maybe we all feel that way
because he is so good at making you feel
like you are the only one in the room, like you are his air.

And when there's all this talk about what Black men are not,
I think about all he is. Marvel that somehow our mother knew
that naming him King would make him into one.

Turning Seventeen

Seventeen is all about burgers at Red Robin with baskets and baskets of unlimited steak fries. Sleepovers at Chanesa's, who lives just a few blocks away, close enough to run back and get something if I forget it. Seventeen is all about R&B-sounding gospel: Dawkins & Dawkins, Virtue, Commissioned. Songs to make you groove *and* feel closer to God. Seventeen is all about gospel-sounding R&B: Jodeci, Aaron Hall, Blackstreet. Songs to make you grind and get closer to your high school crush. Seventeen is all about the mix of caramel & cheese popcorn from Joe Brown's at Lloyd Center Mall, window shopping, and dreaming of the day when I'll be able to buy anything I want. Grown enough to be out without an adult but not too grown that I don't have to check in with my momma, tell her where I am, when I'll be back. At seventeen I learn how to fry fish, how to listen to the hiccupping oil to know when it's ready. Learn how to make jerk chicken, how to make spicy food flavorful and not just hot, hot, hot, learn how cooking makes you closer to your ancestors, makes their presence tangible long after they are gone. Seventeen is all about adults asking, *Where are you going to college?* and *What's next?* and *Who do you want to be?* Seventeen is all about pretending to have it all figured out. Seventeen is about never admitting that even though my dreams are big, big, big, they do not overshadow my fears of missing home and family and friends. They do not overshadow my fear of failing and disappointing all the people who are waiting to see what I become. Seventeen is all about never admitting that the very thing that excites me, terrifies me.

How to Survive Your Teen Years

Remember these days won't last forever. There will come a time when today will be a memory so don't hold too tightly to your failures or successes, they will fade and you will experience many more skies rising. Know this, even when you don't feel this: Your heart is as strong as it is fragile. It will shatter a thousand and one times but always it can heal, if you let it. Trust time to do what it does best. Time heals and teaches, restores and smooths out the rugged edges, slowly—always slowly. Let your joy be big and all-consuming. Laugh a laugh full of rage, the kind of laugh that tells your worry, your sorrow, your grief, *I will survive this // I have survived that // I will survive more.* Don't chase after the ones who leave, turn around and see all the ones who stayed. Hold on to the people who return the love you give. Do not let the words *thank you* be strangers to your tongue. Be a best friend to yourself. Be an enemy only to injustice, to hate. Have a playlist at the ready for every mood, every situation. Be comfortable dancing in a crowded room. Be comfortable dancing in front of the mirror all by yourself. Be your own hype crew. Don't merely dream of who you want to become, be the person you dream to be.

An Etheree for Moving On

Trust
yourself
to know when
it's time to leave
people, places, things.
Staying too long stunts growth,
fosters bitterness, regret.
Around the corner there is more.
Keep going, keep going, keep going.
Sometimes, the one blocking the path is you.

Wield Your Laughter

like the weapon it is.
Flaunt it in the face of your fears.
Cock your head back,
slap your knee,
howl, cackle,
be too loud,
be high-pitched,
be deep bellow,
let the tears fall,
let the belly ache,
let breath escape your lungs,
let your shoulders shake,
let your cheeks turn red.
This is how you mend,
how you endure,
how you hold on to joy
while you wait for happiness.

When Tomorrow Comes

Be the one whose laugh
sounds like the wings of a million birds.
Laugh louder and longer
than anyone in the room.

I want to see you forgiving.
Want you letting go and emptying yourself
of all that's weighing you down.

Want your hands lifted and cupped
ready to receive the downpour.

I want you fully bloomed and fragrant.
Want you succulent and lush.

I want you to be moon.
Stay, stay. No matter who is shining next to you
blocking your shine. Stay, stay.

Yes, I want you to be moon.
A sliver of your light is more than enough.
Always, someone somewhere sees you.

Sisterhood Haiku, III

Gather the women,
the truth-tellers, the wise ones.
Always keep them close.

What I Know About Rain

Don't let the metaphors and platitudes fool you.
Sometimes it is not about the flowers that are coming,
the silver lining, the promised rainbow.

Sometimes the sky is just too dark
and the storm rages for days with no glimmer of sun
and the wind roars and destroys the fragile flowers
that bloomed after the last season of rain.

Sometimes rain blurs your vision,
drenches and consumes you.
Sometimes there is no warning,
no buildup, no prediction of what's to come.
Sometimes rain falls on a sunny day,
a dumping of sorrow
just when you waved goodbye to the clouds.

Sometimes rain is just rain.
Sometimes you have to wait it out,
find a safe space, protection,
a haven, a refuge,
places to comfort and warm you.

Sometimes the lesson is not about the storm
but shelter from it.

Hiraeth*
after Margaret Walker's "Sorrow Home"

My roots are tangled in Marley's dreads.
I was nurtured in the womb of an oak tree.
Thunder and lightning and storm know me well.
I belong to the rose bush. Its thorn and petal, its leaf and stem.

I am not brownstone or skyscraper,
yellow taxi or suffocated sidewalk.
I am not made for squeezing in and out.

I want porch swing and backyard. Want
Pacific Ocean around my corner, mountain at my back.
Want patois on tongue, drum in hips, coconut oil saturating hair.

Oh, Jamaica, can I call you home
even though I only know you
through Grandma's hand-me-down tales?

Oh, Portland**, you town of beauty, of ghosts,
where Tallahatchie waters flood into Columbia River,
drowning Emmett and every boy and girl from Vanport.
Don't you know the past has a way of pricking memory,
like thorn to thumb, unexpectedly?

*Hiraeth: a Welsh word that has no exact English translation. It speaks to the longing for home—not in a simplified homesick way but a deep yearning for the place where your roots are. It's a mixture of nostalgia, grief, and wistfulness for the place of your past. Hiraeth is also described as sorrow because home (past or present) isn't the place it should have been.

**Portland is called The City of Roses.

Black Like Me

and suddenly everyone will see
how Black i am.

black like collard greens & salted meat simmering on a stove.
black like hot water cornbread & iron skillets,
like juke joints & fish fries.
black like soul train lines & the electric slide
at weddings and birthdays.
black like vaseline on ashy knees, like beads decorating braids.
black like cotton fields & soul-cried spirituals.

my skin is black

like red kool-aid, red soda, the red blood
of the lynched and assassinated & that ethiopian man
those skinheads kill with a baseball bat
when i am in the fifth grade.

i am as Black as he was.
my science teacher knows this. she sees
my black and is blind to my brilliance.
can't believe i pass the test with an A
when all the white kids fail

and when she says to the white students,
"you ought to be ashamed of yourselves..."
what she really wants to say is, "i can't believe this Black girl
is smarter than you."

all the white kids look at me
and this is when we learn that the colors of our shells
come with expectations.

i stop being good
at science & math.

my english teacher gives me books & journals
and i read and write the world
as it is, as i want it to be.
i read past my black blues, discover that i am Black
like benjamin banneker & george washington carver,
Black like margaret walker & fannie lou hamer

i am not just slave & despair.
i am struggle & triumph. i learn
to live my life in the searching, in the quest:

can i be Black & brilliant?
can i be jazz & gospel, hip-hop & classical?
can i be christian & accepting?
can i be big & beautiful?

can i be Black like me?
can anyone see me?

Black with a Capital B

*"It seems like such a minor change, black versus Black,"
The Times's National editor, Marc Lacey, said. "But for many people
the capitalization of that one letter is the difference between a color
and a culture." —The New York Times, July 5, 2020*

Betrayed
Bound
Beaten
Bruised
Battered
Bloody
Broken
Belittled
Banned
Blue

Boisterous
Beautiful
Bright
Brave
Brilliant
Budding
Blooming
Breathtaking
Buoyant
Boundless

This is How You Ride a Horse
Rose Festival, 1996
Portland, Oregon

You act like you have been on one
many, many times
because all the 16-year-old white girls have.
Many, many times.
And not the horses of the carousel
with their forever smiles.

You remind yourself that this horse
weighs tons. He will not buckle
under your plump legs once you straddle him.

Get on.
Ride slow.

Close your eyes and imagine your hair
not weighed down by Royal Crown hair grease.
Imagine it galloping on your shoulders.

Don't think about the white-gowned men
riding horses and torching the South.

Don't try to understand the root of your fear
of horses, of dogs.

Become brave enough to learn
how to swim. Swim every day.

Block out your soul's whisper.
It only wants to remind you
that even the tiniest fish
has witnessed bloody tides,
has feasted on Black flesh.

Knock, Knock
for Renisha McBride

Black girls seeking help
can't knock on doors at nighttime
or else they could die
and by die I mean be killed
mistaken for breaking in

(even though intruders don't knock,
scream or announce themselves
or cry out for help
or beg for mercy)

how tragic a world
where Black girls long for Heaven

long for pearly gates to open wide
when they knock, knock, knock
on Heaven's door,
pray God sees his reflection in them

and welcomes them in

A Pantoum for Breonna Taylor

And like all Black women, all you wanted was rest.
Breonna, whose name means noble, exalted one.
Breonna, whose name is an anthem in our throats.
We grieve your possibility, your every about-to.

Breonna, whose name means noble, exalted one.
Breonna, who reminded us that Black women
    are not even safe in our sleep.
We grieve your possibility, your every about-to.
We love you like a play-cousin, love you like you belonged to us.

Breonna, who reminded us that Black women
    are not even safe in our sleep.
We lift your memory, high, high.
We love you like a play-cousin, love you like you belong to us.
Love you because you were like every Black woman—
    so regular, so majestic, all at once.

We lift your memory, high, high.
Breonna, whose name is an anthem in our throats.
Love you because you were like every Black woman—
    so regular, so majestic, all at once.
And like all Black women, all you wanted was rest.

A Tanka for Michelle Obama

Around the way girl,
elegance personified,
let our love heal you.
Know we will never forget
your sacrifice, grit, your grace.

soundtrack for the revolution

a song of lamenting & repentance.
a jazz bop & of course the blues.
play the songs that have no words
so our hearts mourn without influence.

there must be a gospel hymn
for the valleys low & also a jubilee
because there will be, has to be, dancing.

has to be a song that makes our feet
write a new map, a way out
with no bridge for returning
because this new day has come.

and so sing loud
the lyrics that rhyme and riddle
their way to freedom.

sing loud the audacious melodies
that make demands and keep promises.
welcome the drum's solo.
she will lead the way, she will.

let the organ play its Sunday chords,
casting out & cleansing & renewing.

and if you can't sing,
offer your tears,
sacrifice your laugh,
know your whole being
is a harmony of all that's happened
and all that is to come.

Love It All

Love the roundness of your belly
Love your right eye that is smaller than the left
Love your hair on a not-good hair day
Love the celestial patterns eczema tattoos on your skin
Love the itch that crawls slowly, then sprints into burn
Love the hair under your arms
Love the hair on your legs
Love yourself unperfumed & unprimed & unpolished
Love every curve and the flat parts too

Love every mess-up and all the times you could have been better
Love all the times you tried and failed
Love all the embarrassment and all the blunders

Love the rain as much as the sun
Love the wonderings as much as the answers
Love the tears too
Love how love is unpredictable
Love how love breaks you and heals you
Love how love has the greatest expectation
Love how love asks you to rise, love how
love always pushes you to do the impossible

Phenomenon

I have no Black Girl Magic
to give today.

Today, I am regular.
Not insufficient,
not more than enough.
Just me. Just right.

I am hair bonnet,
chipped nail polish, and unpolished toes.

I am morning breath
and crusted eyes and no makeup at all.

And all I have is the lullaby
my momma sang to me
about a mockingbird and a diamond ring
that in real life she never could afford.

And all I have is this history tied around my neck
haunting and hyping me.
All I have is the resilience I inherited.

And all I have is this drum in my chest
beating, thumping, reminding me
that I have survived all my yesterdays.

The magic is all ways me.
The miracle is that I even exist at all.